Maui and the Big Fish

A Polynesian Creation Myth

Retold by Barbara Ker Wilson

Illustrated by Frané Lessac

FRANCES LINCOLN

Long ago when the world was new, before any of the islands of the Pacific Ocean had been created, Maui was born.

His mother thought her newborn baby was dead: sorrowfully she wrapped him in a *tapa* cloth and cast him upon the sea for the waves to carry away.

But the great god Tama looked down from the sky, saw Maui floating on the waves and scooped him up from the sea.

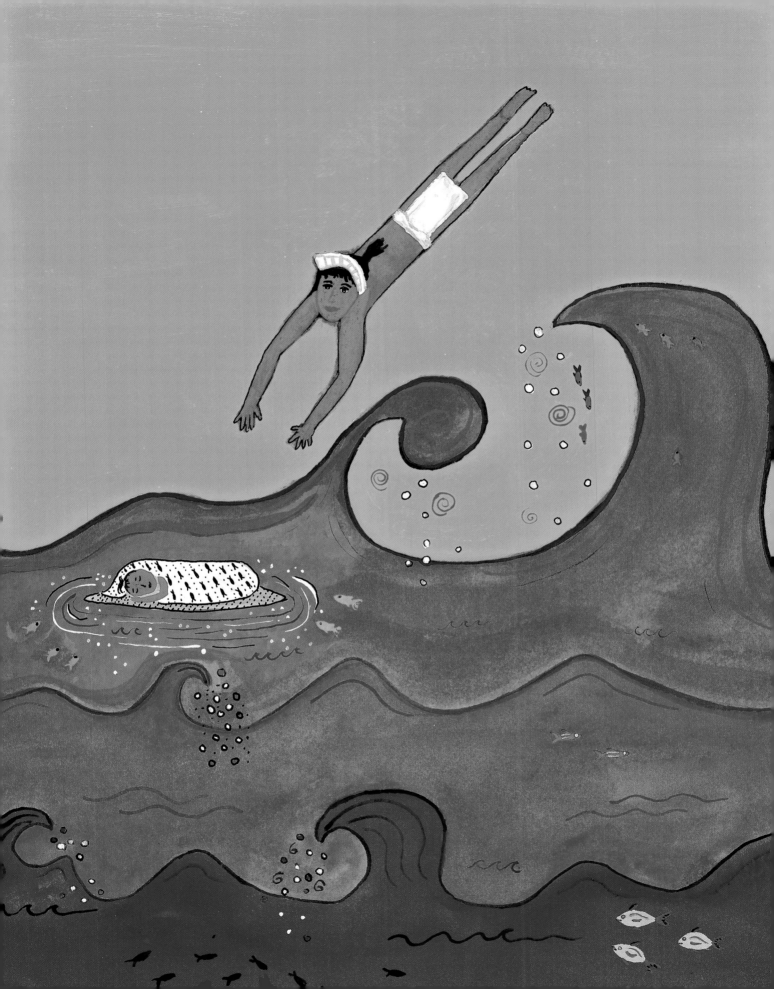

The great god Tama took Maui down to
the underworld, where all the gods lived.
    As Maui grew up, he learned all there is
to know about magic.
    Tama told Maui how he had been rescued
from the sea, and Maui wondered what it would
be like to live on the earth with his mother.

One day Maui wriggled up on to the earth. Singing
a magic chant, he changed himself into a pigeon
and flew across the sky until he found his mother's
house. Then he changed himself back into a little
boy again.

"Who are you?" his mother asked the strange
little boy with a black tuft of hair on top of his head.

"I am the son you cast into the sea. The great god
Tama rescued me."

"My little Maui!" His mother folded him in her arms.
"I shall call you Maui-tikitiki – Maui topknot!"

But when Maui's mother introduced him to
his brothers, they looked down at him scornfully.

Maui's mother told her four big sons to take
Maui-tikitiki with them when they went fishing
in their canoe. The brothers were not pleased ...
His eldest brother said, "Maui is too small. He will
never catch a fish."

"He will get in the way," said the next brother.
"He will upset the canoe," said the third brother.
"He will be sea-sick!" jeered the fourth.

But little Maui-tikitiki didn't listen to them. He was thinking of a plan to give his brothers the biggest surprise of their lives!

Next day Maui-tikitiki's big brothers left home
while he was still in bed. As they launched their
canoe and paddled away, they laughed to think
how easily they had left their little brother behind.

But Maui-tikitiki was not asleep. Although his eyes
were tightly shut, he knew exactly what was going on.
But he had two important things to do before he went
out fishing with his brothers.

First Maui-tikitiki wriggled underground to fetch
his magic fish-hook.

When he wriggled up again, he went to the trees that
grew behind his mother's house and stripped the layers
from each tree until he had a big pile of leaf-stalks.
Singing a magic chant, he pounded them with a stone
to separate the fibres, then twisted the fibres together.
He made the strongest, longest fishing-line in all the world!

At first light next morning, while his brothers
were still snoring away in bed, Maui-tikitiki got up
and wrapped his new fishing line around his body,
with one end attached to his magic fish-hook.

   He went down to the shore. Singing a magic chant,
he changed himself into a dragonfly so that his footprints
would not betray him, and flew over the beach to the canoe.
Then he changed himself back again and hid beneath
the prow of the canoe.

   Soon he heard his brothers arrive, singing:

> *"Paddle the canoe!*
>   *Paddle down the tide with the wind behind us!*
>   *Journey out to the far, deep sea*
>   *Where the big fish await us!"*

Maui-tikitiki stayed hidden as his brothers paddled out to sea. He whispered a magic chant to take the canoe further away from the land than they had ever ventured before. Then he came out of his hiding-place.

"How did you get here?" the first brother exclaimed. He pointed to the stern of the canoe. "Stay down there, out of our way."

The four brothers cast their lines and hauled in a huge catch of fish.

"I can fish too!" Maui-tikitiki shouted. But at that moment he realised that he had forgotten to collect worms to bait his magic fish-hook.

When his brothers refused to give him any of their bait, Maui-tikitiki grew angry. He beat his fist on the side of the canoe so hard that he cut his hand. Seeing the cut gave him an idea. He wiped a tiny drop of blood on to his magic fish-hook, then cast his line into the sea.

His brothers laughed. "Look at little Maui, trying to catch a fish with a drop of blood!" they shouted scornfully.

Suddenly Maui-tikitiki felt his fishing-line whistle
through his fingers. His magic fish-hook had caught
something!

A gigantic sting-ray leapt through the water.
Maui-tikitiki held on to the line with all his strength,
while his four brothers huddled in the stern.

"Cut the line! We shall all drown!" they shouted. But Maui-tikitiki held fast, and after a while the sting-ray began to weaken. Finally it plunged to the bottom of the ocean, defeated. Then Maui-tikitiki's brothers helped him to pull it up ... until at last it lay on top of the water.

By now the four brothers realised that little
Maui-tikitiki possessed magic power. As they
paddled on through the ocean, Maui-tikitiki
caught five more fishes – a huge *bonito*,
a magnificent porpoise, an enormous swordfish,
a tremendous shark and a vast whale.

   "You're a hero, Maui!" shouted his brothers.

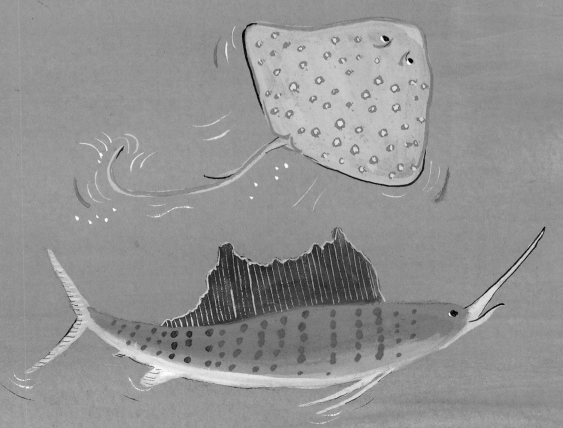

Before their very eyes, each fish turned into an island.
To this day, the islands are known as Maui, Molokai,
Kuaii, Hawaii, Oahu and Lanai.

And when the tale of that great fishing
expedition became known, the people said Maui
deserved a new name. He became Maui-tinihanga,
"Maui of the Thousand Tricks", throughout
all the islands of Polynesia.